Witch-i

Other **Witch-in-Training** *titles*

Flying Lessons

Spelling Trouble

Charming or What?

Brewing Up

Broomstick Battles

Witch-in-
Training
Witch Switch

Maeve Friel

Illustrated by Nathan Reed

HarperCollins *Children's Books*

First published in Great Britain by HarperCollins *Children's Books* 2005
HarperCollins *Children's Books* is a division of HarperCollins*Publishers* Ltd
77-85 Fulham Palace Road, Hammersmith, London W6 8JB

The HarperCollins *Children's Books* website address is
www.harpercollinschildrensbooks.co.uk

1 3 5 7 9 8 6 4 2

Text © Maeve Friel 2005
Illustrations © Nathan Reed 2005

ISBN 0 00 718525 1

The author and illustrator assert the moral right
to be identified as author and illustrator of the work.

Printed and bound in England by
Clays Ltd, St Ives plc

Chapter One

The sky was black with witches on brooms, all flying in the same direction as Jessica. They turned left when she turned left. They turned right when she turned right. When she began to descend to the High Street, the

broom riders started to descend too.

"Are they following me?" Jessica wondered. "Or are they just going shopping in Miss Strega's?"

Miss Strega's hardware shop, where Jessica was doing her witch training lessons, was the most popular witches' shop in the whole world. It always had the most up-to-date Brewing ingredients, Spell Books, Charms and brooms, but it was still unusual to see so many customers arriving all at once.

Of course, Jessica was the only one who saw the witches and their brooms. Ordinary People never noticed Miss Strega's customers flying hither and thither. They didn't even see the old hardware shop, for it was a secret "In Between" place, protected by a "For Witches' Eyes Only" Spell. Miss Strega didn't want nosy parkers snooping around, making trouble for Witches World Wide.

As Jessica came nearer the shop, she saw that there was a long queue outside the

door, so she flew on to the roof, climbed through the dormer window, Zoomed through the attic trapdoor and landed with a thump on the shop counter.

Miss Strega peered over her glasses.

"I expect you have a reason for coming in through the roof, Jessica?"

"I was avoiding the crowds, Miss Strega. There are hundreds of witches outside."

Miss Strega clapped her hands. "Ticketyboo. I'm offering free potion this evening so I hoped lots of customers would turn up."

"You're having a free potion evening? What about my class?"

"Doing the Witch Switch? Yes, we will have a class later. But I thought it might be interesting to have some old friends drop in first" – she gave a little giggle – "for a change."

"Doing the Witch Switch? What's that?"

Miss Strega cupped her long chin in her hand as if she were considering Jessica's question carefully. "It's a bit like shape changing, I suppose, but more extreme."

Jessica groaned. She had never been any good at changing the shapes of things, with or without a wand. Once she had sort-of-accidentally transformed Miss Strega into a wasp, but then Miss Strega had got her own back and turned Jessica into a large pumpkin. It was scary being a pumpkin, thinking that someone might come along and carve you up for a Halloween lantern or turn you into a pie.

"Is that a good idea, Miss Strega?" she asked. "I'm quite happy with the shape I am. And I'd rather not have people eating bits of me when I'm not myself. Remember Felicity?"

Felicity, Miss Strega's cat, had once turned into a ginger cat-shaped biscuit. She had been snoozing on a Spell Book and a Transformation Spell had slipped into her dreams. Unfortunately, before she was changed back into a cat, both Miss Strega and Berkeley, Jessica's nightingale mascot, had nibbled little bits of her. Poor Felicity still looked a bit ragged around the ears.

"Fiddlesticks!" Miss Strega snorted. "The Witch Switch is something all witches do: it's as traditional as Brewing or Flying – it's useful in emergencies, it's handy if you're on a spying mission and it can be good fun. Now, open the door, poppet."

As soon as Jessica turned the Closed notice on the door to Open, witches and hags of every shape and size began to elbow their way in.

"Four packets of troll squeals," one shouted. "Two pokes of rompedenti biscuits."

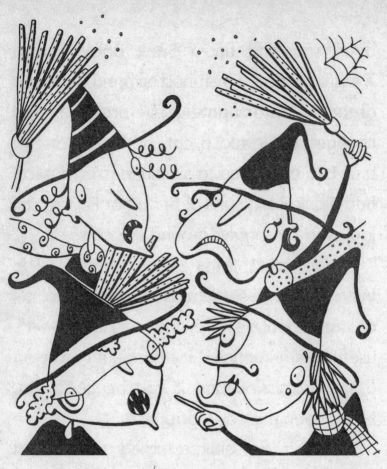

"I want one of those dragons' teeth that you can plant to grow your own hero."

Jessica was just about to whizz off to the ingredient drawers when she felt a sharp tug on the back of her cape.

"I think you'll find I'm first in line, young lady," snarled a very pushy hag. "I would like a large tub of gnats' spittle and a carton of dry goats' poo."

"No!" screeched another. "I was definitely in front of you."

"No way," howled another. "I got here first!"

Fortunately, at that very moment, Miss Strega began to pass around glasses of colourful potions.

"Drinks, anyone?" she asked sweetly. "Mint Royale? Or would you prefer White Gold?"

After that, no one seemed to care about their turn in the queue any more. Jessica suspected that Miss Strega had been up to her old tricks, adding a spell to her potions so that all the witches wanted to do was spend, spend, spend and cackle, cackle,

cackle. Even Berkeley, who was awfully shy about singing in public, had fallen under a spell. She perched prettily on the handle of the Brewing cauldron and bewitched the customers with her lovely silvery songs.

Jessica, as the witch-in-training, was left to do all the hard work. She fetched ingredients, filled bottles with Walpurga's magic well water, parcelled up new capes and helped load cauldrons full of shopping

on to the backs of brooms.

More and more customers arrived. They stood around, yakking and drinking and cackling their heads off at Miss Strega's old jokes.

The noise was so deafening that Jessica didn't hear the door click.

She was on her knees behind the counter, searching for a Cover of Darkness blanket, when she realised that the shop had gone very, very quiet.

She stood up slowly and peered over the counter.

All the witches had disappeared. There was not a single hag trying on a cape or enjoying a natter with Miss Strega.

On the other hand, an awful lot of cats had appeared from nowhere. They padded across the floor and sprawled on the windowsills. Several were lying on the counter. One or two were even attempting

to climb into the drawers. And where three witches had been sitting gossiping around the Brewing cauldron, there were three life-size garden gnomes that definitely had not been there before.

"Oh my goodness!" exclaimed an unfamiliar voice. "What a lot of cats."

Jessica whirled around. There was an Ordinary Person standing in the doorway!

Chapter Two

Jessica rushed out from behind the counter. "I'm sorry," she croaked, for her mouth had gone completely dry, "we are closed. Miss Strega has already left."

At the same time she was thinking,

blithering batwings, what if some witch flies in on her broomstick while this Ordinary Person is here?

"Tell me," said the Ordinary Person, fixing Jessica with a steely stare, "exactly how many cats do you have?"

Jessica said nothing, but she began to shoo the cats towards the cat flap with the end of her broom.

Miss Strega, help! she prayed.

The problem was that the cats just wouldn't leave. They mewed and howled, scratched and hissed. Some of them arched their backs and refused to budge. Others tried to trip Jessica up by doing figures of eight around her legs. Another big fat black one bolted from behind the counter and upset a teetering pile of cauldrons.

"Oops! That pot missed me by the

pompom of my hood," one of the garden gnomes whispered. "I feel quite faint."

Jessica was flabbergasted. "So that's it! You've all changed into cats and gnomes and left me all alone. It's not fair!"

The Ordinary Person began to walk around. She looked at the jumble of cobwebby mole traps and hurricane lamps in the window. She pursed her lips at the black cauldrons and raised an eyebrow at the heap of broomsticks that the witches had left beside the door.

"They're for brushing up fallen leaves," Jessica muttered as she trailed after her.

The Ordinary Person wasn't listening. She was staring at the three curious garden gnomes whose eyes seemed to follow her as she walked around the room.

"I've never noticed this shop before," she remarked in a very frosty voice, "and that is odd because I work next door in the toy shop."

"Really?" Jessica squeaked.

The Ordinary Person wrinkled her nose. She began to count all the cats: on the counter, stretched out on the shelves, asleep in the cauldrons and peeping out of drawers.

"It's all a bit odd, isn't it? Not to mention smelly."

Jessica's face and ears turned scarlet.

Get out, she thought. *Go away and leave us alone!*

But now the Ordinary Person marched to the drawers at the back of the shop and scrunched her eyes up at their spidery handwritten labels.

"Well, since I'm here I'll have a flea collar, just in case one of these flea-bitten old strays bumps into my little moggie."

"Sorry, we don't sell them."

"Nonsense! There's a drawer here marked Flea Collars. I'll get one myself."

The Ordinary Person went to pull open a drawer that Jessica knew contained a bloodcurdling collection of freaky hollers: WHOOOO! WAAAARGH!

There was no time to lose.

She stomped across the shop, whacking the floor with her broom: left, right, left, right.

"Don't open that! It's empty. We have no flea collars for sale. None at all. Goodbye."

And she practically swept the Ordinary Person out on to the street and banged the door shut.

"Blithering batwings and warty warlocks!"

Behind her, all the stray cats began clambering out of drawers, hopping off the counter and carefully picking their way over the spilled pile of cauldrons.

Suddenly, before you could say moonbeams and marrowbones, the racket started again. Witches cackled. Glasses clinked. Berkeley trilled. And there were all the witches standing around, leaning on their

brooms, trying on capes, leafing through Spell Books and sipping fresh glasses of Midnight Magic.

"Thank you, ladies, for such speedy Switching," said Miss Strega.

"It's years since an Ordinary Person barged in like that."

Jessica rounded on her. "Why did you leave me all alone? We could have been found out!"

"Great honking goose feathers!" Miss Strega snorted. "Calm down, of course we couldn't have been found out. Ordinary People don't see witches. And, anyway, here in the shop we're In Between."

"Well, that Ordinary Person saw me. She managed to get In Between. She was definitely suspicious of all the cauldrons and broomsticks and cats. And she spotted the gnomes' eyes following her. What if she had opened that drawer full of freaky hollers?"

"Don't worry your enchanting little head about her, Jessica. She won't be back. You saw for yourself how put off she was by all the cats." She turned to the witches who had switched to gnomes. "By the way, ladies, thank you for not screaming when that cauldron went flying."

"You're welcome, Miss Strega," they chorused. "You can always rely on us to keep the Witch Switch Promise."

"What about me?" exclaimed Jessica. "I didn't know how to turn myself into a cat or a gnome!"

"There, there," Miss Strega replied, soothingly. "You just need some practice. I told you I was having some friends in for a change – I thought you'd be amused if we all suddenly made a switch. Then the Ordinary Person turned up. That was a lucky coincidence!"

"Very lucky," sniffed Jessica.

One by
one, the last
of Miss Strega's
customers gathered
up their packages and
loaded up their brooms. They
chattered and hugged, promised to
meet for Muncheon and then

Zoomed off through the trapdoor to the
rooftop. The last one had just departed when
once again the door latch clicked.

"Hello," said a second Ordinary Person,
poking her head around the
door. "Those black pots you
have in the window – they'd
be perfect for planting
petunias on my patio – how
much are they?"

"I don't know," Jessica stammered. Miss Strega had vanished again. "I think they're about ten maravedis. Or maybe ten groats…"

The Second Ordinary Person frowned. "Maravedis? Groats?"

Jessica smiled weakly. *Please just go away*, she was thinking.

But the Second Ordinary Person had caught sight of the ingredient drawers at the back wall and strode bossily towards them. The labels swam around.

"Does that say Frog Spawn?" She squinted at the drawers. "And does that one say Teenage Slugs?"

"Frying pans," said Jessica, quickly. "Ten-amp plugs. Miss Strega's handwriting is terrible."

The Second Ordinary Person looked Jessica up and down, from the top of her

aerodynamic flying helmet to the hem of her
black witch's cape.

"Are you in fancy dress?"

Jessica shook her head. Then she nodded
fiercely. "Yes, yes, I am."

"I'll give you ten pounds for this pot," said
the Second Ordinary Person at last. "If it's
more, you can pop in and see me next door
at the estate agent's."

She scooped up one of the witch's cauldrons, slapped a note on the counter and went off, muttering, "Maravedis! Groats! Fancy dress at this time of year? Ridiculous."

Jessica rushed to the door, turned the Open sign to Closed and drew the curtains. Then she marched crossly back to Miss Strega's high stool, where a tiny brown moth was resting.

"Miss Strega, I presume?" she said. "We need to talk."

"Absolutely, my little lamb's lettuce," said the moth, stretching her wings. "Just give me a moment to change."

Chapter Three

When Miss Strega was herself again, Jessica explained that she was worried.

"I think that the For Witches' Eyes Only Spell is wearing off. Ordinary People are slipping through some sort of a hole that lets them see the shop In Between."

Miss Strega cupped her long chin in her hand. "It is unusual to have two unwelcome visitors on one day but, on the other hand, Ordinary People are silly billies.  They don't believe in magic so they don't always see what's in front of their noses."

"Well, I was an Ordinary Person until my birthday so I remember what they're like. Ordinary People don't understand witches. If they realise that you are running a witchy shop right here on the High Street, they'll come and throw eggs and boo and shout and blame you for bad things you didn't do. They'll close the shop down. They might even lock you up in one of their jails."

"But that is where Switching comes in, Jess. At the first sign of people breaking into our space, we turn into something else."

"How?"

Miss Strega looked thoughtful. "The same way that an acorn becomes an oak or an egg becomes a turkey. An egg doesn't need to puzzle over Becoming A Turkey – it just does. A caterpillar doesn't have a Becoming A Butterfly lesson. Switching is the same for us witches. It's just faster. A witch can change instantly into anything she wants to be. "

"Anything?"

"Of course. But switching can be risky too. You have got to be brave to switch; you have got to trust your sister witches. That's why we make the Witch Switch Promise."

Jessica raised an eyebrow.

"Every witch must promise never to scream while another witch has Switched. Otherwise, the Switched witch will be stuck in whatever shape she had turned into."

Jessica looked completely baffled.

"Remember when the cauldrons toppled over and nearly knocked the heads off the garden gnomes? Well, if even one of those gnomes had screamed, we would all have been stuck – locked into cat-ness or gnome-ness."

"For ever?"

Miss Strega shrugged. "Did I ever tell you about my great-aunt Delenda, the one who turned herself into a gargoyle for a dare? Her witch-in-training was so frightened by her ugly stony face, she screamed the house down. Delenda has been stuck under a gutter ever since." Miss Strega shook her head sadly and began to gather up the empty potion glasses. "They say her face is wearing away with all the rainwater pouring down on her."

Jessica wrinkled her nose. She wasn't quite sure whether to believe Miss Strega or not. It might be one of her old jokes. She had certainly never mentioned Great-aunt Delenda before.

"Why don't I demonstrate the Witch Switch?" Miss Strega suggested, brightening up. "Then you can have a go. But first of all, are you ready to make the Witch Switch Promise?"

"I am."

"Do you swear by the yellow toenails of the Rocky Mountain raven never to scream at a switched witch?"

"I do."

"Do you swear by the raucous squawking of the White Peacock always to trust your sister witches?"

"I do."

"Well then," said Miss Strega, "let the Witch Switching begin."

Suddenly she was looming over Jessica in the shape of a long-necked giraffe. "You can be big," she said, "or you can be tiny…" Now she was a little grey mouse on the floor, squeaking in a high voice.

"You can be slippery…" A green snake slithered up on to the counter and looped itself into coils like a tall pile of rope.

"Or you can be spiny…" Miss Strega had become a  porcupine, shaking out her bristles with a loud clack.

"Or feathery…" In a trice, Miss Strega had become a black hen with a silly hairdo, pecking at the crumbs on the floor.

"Or how about leathery?" She Switched into an enormous bull with a ring at the end of her nose. She snorted and drummed her hooves and took up so much room that Jessica was squashed into a corner of the shop.

"You can be hairy..." A very hairy mutt smiled at Jessica from under a blonde fringe and trundled off behind the counter.

"Or scary..." Jessica felt a tap on her shoulder. When

she spun round, there, to her horror, was Shar Pintake, the scariest witch of all and Chief Examiner of Witches World Wide, sucking her teeth  and making that awful breathy noise! Jessica clapped a hand over her mouth to stifle a scream—

Just as Miss Strega Switched back to being Miss Strega again.

"Bravo!" said Jessica, clapping her hands. "Take a bow!"

"Nonsense," said Miss Strega, "there's nothing to it."

"And I didn't scream," said Jessica proudly. "Not even when you Switched to that Shar Pintake lookalike."

"Now it's your turn," said Miss Strega. "Go on, have a go!"

Jessica pondered. "Shall I be big, tiny, slippery, spiny, feathery, leathery, hairy or scary?"

"To start with, why don't you become a cat? In an emergency, a witch's best Switch is a cat. Most Ordinary People rarely notice cats padding about so become a cat and – Hey presto! – you're free to go wherever you like. Most of the cats in the ordinary world are actually witches in disguise."

Jessica thought very hard about the word "cat".

Whiskers sprouted from her cheeks. Her nose twitched. She sniffed. She had never before noticed all the strong smells of the shop, the gingeriness of the rompedenti biscuits that made your teeth fall out, the dusty dryness of owl feathers or the lemony-clove smell of the Brewing cauldron.

Her ears slid up to the top of her head and flickered from side to side. She had never realised how noisy the world was for a cat. Zzzzzzz. A bumblebee trapped in the window

buzzed like an electric drill. Click, click went the big shop clock.

Prroom, prrroom.. Something in her throat was making purring sounds.

 Her skin became furry and sleek, as if she had been tucked up inside cosy all-in-one pyjamas.

Her hands became little pink cushiony paws with long sharp claws. She flicked them out and drew them back in.

She made a great yawn, the way Felicity did, showing Miss Strega a long pink tongue and two rows of formidably sharp teeth.

Most curious of all, she could feel a long tail unfurl behind her.

"Prrrrrooom," she repeated, in a very pleased voice. "I'm a cat."

"There's no denying that," agreed Miss Strega. "And as dandy a cat as ever I've seen. Well done."

Jessica Switched back to being herself. She patted her face to check that everything was in its proper place and she hadn't ended up with whiskers or pointy ears. She peeked under her cloak – phew! – no tail, either.

"That was good fun," said Jessica, grinning, "but Switching into something scary seems to be asking for trouble."

"Oh yes indeedy," Miss Strega agreed. "Switching can be very dangerous if you're with the kind of people who yell and hoot and scream at the least scary thing. Remember Great-aunt Delenda and never forget the Switchers' Promise: No Screaming Allowed."

Chapter Four

A loud crash made Jessica jump. She flew over to the door and peered around the curtain. Up and down the High Street, shops were closing for the night. Shopkeepers were rolling down their metal shutters with tremendous bangs. To her right, someone was heaving a wheelie bin to the edge of the pavement in front of the toy shop.

"It's the FOP!" Jessica gasped. The First Ordinary Person!

The FOP turned to go back into her shop, but something made her stop. She looked up at Miss Strega's creaking shop sign and frowned.

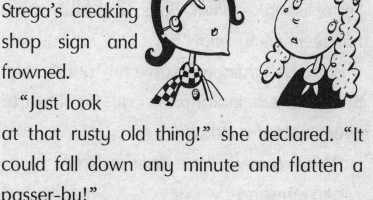

"Just look at that rusty old thing!" she declared. "It could fall down any minute and flatten a passer-by!"

"Absolutely!" said another voice.

Jessica squinted to see who was speaking. It was the SOP, the Second Ordinary Person, rolling *her* wheelie bin on to the pavement outside the estate agent's.

"It's a funny thing," said the FOP to the SOP, "but I had never even noticed we had this shop in between us until this afternoon."

"Me neither," said the SOP, squinting at the lettering of the shop sign. "Miss Strega's Hardware Shop," she read aloud, "established – what does that say? *Nine nineteen* ninety-one?"

Both the Ordinary People tut-tutted. Then they glared indignantly at the scruffy overcrowded window.

"What a mess. It's a disgrace!"

"An eyesore!"

"And overrun with cats!"

"Have you come across the very rude girl in the fancy-dress costume? She almost swept me out of the shop today. She really is like a little witch."

"There's something creepy about the whole setup. I had the feeling I was being watched by three garden gnomes."

"And there's something fishy about those

drawers behind the counter – I can't quite put my finger on it."

"Why don't we have a word with this Miss Strega? We'll tell her she'll have to buck up her ideas, get rid of all those cats, fix that shop sign and sort out all the rubbish in that window… or else!"

"Good idea."

Jessica turned away from the door. "It's getting worse, Miss Strega," Jessica hissed. "The shop is visible to the two Ordinary People at the *same time*. They are coming back *together*."

She was talking to thin air. Miss Strega was nowhere to be seen, but there *was* a long-eared owl gazing down from the curtain pole, slowly moving its head from side to side.

The door latch clicked.

"Miss Strega!" shouted the FOP.

"Anyone here?" bawled the SOP.

At the sound of their voices, the owl swooped down on wide silent wings. "Too-whit, too-woooo," it hooted.

The two Ordinary People shrieked. The owl dipped and dived and wheeled over their heads. Its long talons dangled above them as they rushed around in circles, flapping their arms. They tripped over cauldrons and knocked into garden forks. They howled at Jessica. The owl hooted nonstop. Felicity crashed noisily out through the cat flap.

"Do something about that owl, you silly little WITCH!" shouted the FOP.

Oh no! Had the FOP guessed she was not just in fancy dress?

Jessica screamed.

The two Ordinary People wrestled the door open, screeching like banshees.

When they had gone, a solitary white feather floated down from the ceiling and landed at Jessica's feet.

Jessica's heart stopped when she realised what she had done.

"Miss Strega, where are you? I didn't mean to scream. Come back!"

But Miss Strega was nowhere to be seen.

Jessica sank to the floor and buried her head in her hands. She had made so many mistakes. She had not Switched. She should have turned into a cat as soon as she heard the strangers talking outside. But worst of all, she had broken the Witch Switch Promise, and now Miss Strega was gone, locked into being an owl. She must have flown out after the Ordinary Persons and was probably hooting around the roofs of the High Street. Poor Miss Strega. Jessica pictured her, all alone and sad, hunting for mice in the park instead of having a jolly tasty Muncheon up on the chimneypots.

Jessica sniffed and wiped her nose on her sleeve.

"Come on, Berkeley, let's take to the sky and keep flying until we find her."

She was just about to mount her broomstick and go up to the roof when she again heard voices on the High Street.

No! The two Ordinary People were outside.

"We've got a problem," said one to the other. "It looks as if this so-called Miss Strega has abandoned her shop. It must be crawling with creatures."

"It's time to shut the whole place down," said the other, "and do something about that wild child."

Chapter Five

Jessica grabbed her broom and shot up through the attic trapdoor. She Zoomed out of the dormer window and landed on a chimneypot. From there, she peered into the darkness and called out in a low urgent

whisper: "Miss Strega, are you there? Too-woo? Too-woo?"

No answer came.

All night long, Jessica flitted along the rooftops, searching under eaves and calling down chimneys. She peered into nest boxes and poked at the leaves in the gutters. It was no use.

Miss Strega, the best witch trainer ever, had vanished – and it was all Jessica's fault.

She tearfully turned her broom homeward.

To think that she would never again hear Miss Strega say "moonrays and marrowbones". Never be able to have midnight feasts of Muncheon and Cold Smelly Vole Brew with her again. Never be able to hold her hand and Vault over the moon.

Suddenly Jessica froze in mid-flight. Her face turned as pale as an owl's egg.

She had completely forgotten about the Witches World Wide association. What would they say when they heard the news that Jessica had broken the Witch Switch Promise? When they knew that their Number One Witch Shopkeeper had grown very long ear tufts and feathers, and that she was, in fact, a fine specimen of Asio otus, the long-eared owl?

Jessica wondered if she should go to Coven Garden and ask Shar Pintake for help? The very thought of it made her feel sick. No. She would have to find her sweet, lovely, funny Miss Strega before anyone else found out. But how?

"Chirrup," whistled Berkeley, suddenly popping up out of her pocket and giving an encouraging trill. "Chirrup."

Jessica wiped her nose.

"You're quite right, Berkeley," she sniffed. "I *am* training to be a witch, after all. I *will* find Miss Strega. I just need time to think."

She stroked her chin wisely, the way that Miss Strega always did.

Then she flew home to read every Spell Book she could lay her hands on.

Early the next morning, Jessica flew back to the hardware shop. The two Ordinary People were already standing outside, looking cross as usual. One of them was banging on the door and clutching a brown envelope.

Jessica, wrapped up in her Super-duper Deluxe Guaranteed-Invisibility-When-You-Need-It cape, perched on the shop sign and watched them.

"I told you there would be no one here," snapped the First Ordinary Person.

"Fine!" barked the Second Ordinary Person. "But we can still leave the letter."

"There's no letter box! Just throw it through the cat flap." And they flounced off, fuming, to their own shops.

When they had gone, Jessica let herself in. At the click of the door latch, Felicity turned around from her overflowing bowl of Kattifer's Krunchies and gave her an orange wink.

"How can you eat that horrid stuff? Don't you even care that Miss Strega has vanished?" Jessica scolded.

When Felicity didn't answer, Jessica locked the door, picked up the envelope, climbed on to the counter and read the letter.

Dear Miss Strega,

Your shop is a danger to public health; it is full of wild cats and birds. It is (to be frank) smelly.

Your creaky shop sign is hanging off the wall and could fall and take someone's head off.

Your shop window display is a dusty, cobwebby, shabby disgrace to the High Street.

Unless you respond by midday, we intend to take matters into our own hands.

Your neighbours

"Moonrays and marrowbones!" exclaimed Jessica. "I had better get on with my Reappearing Miss Strega Spell on the double."

She fetched a cauldron and set to work. She had already picked a spell called Brewing in the Round. *Spelling Made Easy* said it was "the perfect remedy when everything is wrong and nothing is right". In that case, Jessica told Felicity and Berkeley, it could definitely bring Miss Strega home.

She began to fetch all the ingredients she needed from Miss Strega's drawers and cupboards and set everything out in little saucers on the counter. Every single thing was round. There was the dried eye of a crocodile,

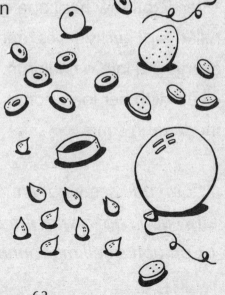

a scrape of fish scales and a dragon's egg. There were oodles of O's, a cupful of cherry stones and a pint of fairy tears. There were three balloons, two pearl buttons and one gold ring. Finally, Jessica rummaged in her pocket for the lucky charm pebble that she had picked up on Pelagia's beach, the one that had a perfect round hole in it, and placed that on the counter too.

The shop crackled with magic.

Jessica threw her cape over her shoulders, rolled up her sleeves and began to pour everything into a cauldron. As she Mingled it all up with her long-eared owl's feather, she made up a song.

"Can you see what I'm Brewing?
Do you know what I'm doing?
Can you smell my round soup

As it wafts round the shop?
Can you see my round gloop
Bubble up to the top?"

She stirred and stirred – left and right, round and round – made figures of eight and smacked the rim of the cauldron three times.

Clouds of round bubbles floated around the shop.

Round things rose up through the fizzing mixture and winked as she sang.

"By the roundness of round things that go round and round,
You went away once but now you are found."

She gave the cauldron a final smack.

There was a knock at the door. Jessica's smile was wide enough to hook over her ears. She laid down her feather and ran to let Miss Strega in.

But no! It was not Miss Strega. It was the FOP and the SOP who were banging on the door. The wrong people had reappeared! So much for the Brewing in the Round Spell!

Just in the nick of time, Jessica Switched to a cat.

Chapter Six

The FOP and the SOP thumped loudly on the door. They peered through the window and called Miss Strega's name.

Jessica sat beside Felicity on the counter and paid no attention. It was quite pleasant being a cat again, thought Jessica (even the

Kattifer's Krunchies smelled quite tasty).
While she waited for her horrible neighbours
to go away, she carefully cleaned behind her
ears and had A Good Think.

Her Good Think went like this. *Somehow,*
she thought, *I am going to have to make
the pesky FOP and SOP forget all about the
shop. They must forget they have seen it.
They must forget they have been in it. They
must forget about the owl on the loose and
the cats, the shabby windows and the
creaking sign, the flea collars and where
they bought the pot to put petunias on their
patio. They must forget all thoughts about
broomsticks and witches and garden
gnomes with swivelling eyes. Then, when I
have got rid of them once and for all, I will
be able to concentrate on getting Miss
Strega safely back home and she can put*

the For Witches' Eyes Only Spell back on the shop.

"So," she told Berkeley and Felicity when the banging had stopped and the Ordinary People had gone away, "I am going to have a tea party. I am going to invite the Ordinary People to pop in for tea and a chat."

Felicity waggled her long eyebrows. Berkeley whistled nervously.

"Don't worry, I have a plan," said Jessica, "but I will need your help. Felicity, I want you to sit on the windowsill of the toy shop. Berkeley, I want you to perch on our shop sign. If the FOP or the SOP come anywhere near, you must both start meowing and whistling as loudly as you can. I don't want them barging in before I'm ready."

"Hu-eeet," agreed Berkeley.

Felicity waved a ragged ear.

"Right," said Jessica, Switching back into herself, "off you go. I have got to prepare a very special tea and get changed."

The plan swung into action.

Jessica wrote two notes and popped one under the door of both the estate agent's and the toy shop.

> Miss Bella Strega requests
> your company for tea at shop
> closing time.

Berkeley and Felicity took up their posts.

Jessica reached for her cauldron and *The Little Book of Teatime Treats* by Delia Catessen.

"I hope this works better than that useless Brewing in the Round. Toes and fingers crossed."

At seven o'clock precisely, the FOP appeared at the doorway of her shop. Felicity set up a deafening mewing. The SOP appeared at the doorway of the estate agent's. Berkeley trilled at the top of her voice.

The FOP and the SOP met under Miss Strega's shop sign. Together, they banged on Miss Strega's door.

Inside the shop, Jessica checked her appearance in the cloak cupboard mirror and straightened her hat.

"Quite a good lookalike," she said, peering over her half-moon glasses.

There was another bang at the door.

She threw it wide open.

The two Ordinary People stood there, hands on their hips, ready to give Miss Strega a piece of their minds.

"Is that your cat on my windowsill?" said the FOP.

"Has this odd bird got anything to do with you?" demanded the SOP.

"Do come in," said Jessica.

The two Ordinary People looked doubtfully at their hostess, for of course they had never seen Miss Strega before. She was awfully strange, no taller than a ten-year-old child, and all wrapped up from head to toe in a strange black dress. Her glasses were perched on the end of her nose and

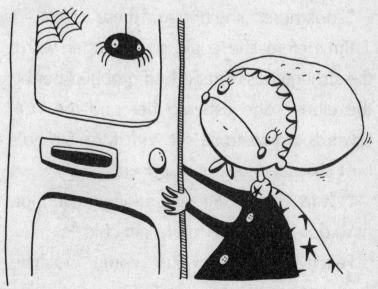

73

she was wearing a kind of bonnet that had gone out of fashion a hundred years ago.

The FOP turned to the SOP.

"Witch?" she mouthed silently.

But the SOP had wandered off to the drawers at the back of the shop. The letters of the spidery handwritten labels swam around. *Teenage Slugs. Snail's Antennae.* She squinted again. *Ten-amp Plugs. Ten-inch Nails.*

"Look here," she began, "these letters—"

But before she could say another word, the strange Miss Strega had grabbed her by the elbow. She ushered her and the FOP towards a low table set with Miss Strega's best china teacups and saucers.

"Chop, chop," she said, raising the teapot. "We don't want the tea to get cold."

Felicity, who had just come crashing

through the cat flap, stopped in her tracks and stared at the Miss Strega lookalike. Her tail stood straight on end in surprise. Jessica winked.

As soon as the Ordinary People had sat down, the First Ordinary Person rummaged in a carrier bag and pulled out a thick notebook. She licked the end of a pencil and turned over a page.

"We, that is to say, the two of us, have a little list of complaints."

"Milk or lemon?"

"Milk. Perhaps first we could talk about the dangerous shop sign…"

"Sugar?"

"And we're very, very worried about vermin—" the Second Ordinary Person began.

"Sugar?"

"Just one lump."

"Let's not forget the stray cats…"

"And of course something will have to be done about the owl that's on the loose."

"A biscuit?"

"The window display is simply unacceptable—"

"Chocolate digestive or wafer?"

"That wild child is totally out of control. Is she some kind of relative of yours?"

"And pray tell us, exactly what kind of business are you running here?" The SOP squinted again at the drawer labels. "Does that really say *Gnat's Spittle*?"

The Miss Strega lookalike tapped her nose. "Tea first," she said. "There will be lots of time later for our little chat." She raised her cup.

The two Ordinary People nervously picked up their cups. They each took a tiny sip. Then they took another and another.

"Mmm," they said together, smacking their lips. "That's delicious tea. Any chance of a top-up?"

"Now, what was it you wanted to talk to me about?" asked Jessica when they had finished their second cup.

The First Ordinary Person looked bewildered. She gazed around the shop as if, suddenly, she hadn't a clue where she was or how or why she had arrived there. She slowly replaced her cup on the saucer.

"What – what was it we were talking about? I seem to have forgotten why... how... er... where... um..." She stood up.

The Second Ordinary Person looked equally baffled. She too set down her teacup and looked at her watch.

"Just look at the time," she stammered. "What am I thinking of? I have a train to catch."

And they both scuttled off, without even saying goodbye or thank you for the lovely tea.

"Phew," said Jessica, removing her bonnet and half-moon glasses. "That Tea of

Forgetfulness Spell is magic. It really works. Now, the next part of the plan is to find Miss Strega."

"Well," said a familiar voice, "look no further – here I am."

Chapter Seven

Jessica wheeled around.

There, sitting on her usual place on the high stool behind the counter, was the real Miss Strega. Unfortunately, she was still an owl with amazing ear tufts.

"By the toot of my midnight hoot, I think you've done it. You need never worry your enchanting little head about that pair of nincompoops. They won't give us any more trouble."

"You're back!" shouted Jessica. She hurtled across the room to give Miss Strega a hug.

"Hang on!" shouted Miss Strega. "I don't want you breaking one of my wings." She fluttered off her stool and flapped on to the curtain pole. "Anyway, I've been here all the time, watching you."

Jessica was shocked. "You have? Oh Miss Strega, I am so sorry for breaking the Witch Switch Promise. I made a Round Brew for you to reappear in your proper shape, but..." Her shoulders drooped. "It didn't work. If only I'd Switched when the Ordinary People first came back. Then none of this would have happened. I'm just not very good at shape changing. I never have been."

Miss Strega flapped back down to her stool again. Her head swivelled round owlishly.

"You managed to do a *lookalike* me."

"I just dressed up as you," said Jessica. "I wouldn't have dared Switch into you. But," she went on, "I've been thinking. Being an owl isn't the end of the world. You can come and live with me. I'll look after you, I promise. What do owls like to eat? Dead mice? I'm sure that Felicity will give you hunting tips. And Berkeley too of course. I'll make you a Brew of Cold Smelly Voles every single night. We'll be all right, just the four of us. I'm sure life as an owl is really great fun, the way you can move your head nearly all the way round in a circle and the way you can vomit up little parcels of fur, and of course being wise must be very interesting—"

"Stop wittering, Jessica, and listen," interrupted Miss Strega. "I didn't get where I am today without learning how to undo a botched Witch Switch. But I stayed as an owl

84

for you to see what happens if you break the Witch Switch Promise. Now, I'd like you to do one thing for me to show that you will never forget it again."

"Anything you say, Miss Strega."

"You must do another Witch Switch."

"What would you like me to be? I can be big or I can be tiny, I can be slippery or spiny, feathery or leathery, hairy or..." Jessica hesitated. "...*furry,*"

"You've left out the most important one!"

"Do you mean scary?" Jessica frowned. That was the one thing she didn't want to be. Being scary was asking for trouble.

Miss Strega nodded. "Yes, be scary."

"Do you promise not to scream or be afraid?"

"I promise."

Jessica thought SCARY.

What was scary was thinking about being stuck for ever in the wrong shape. What was really scary was wondering if Miss Strega would keep her promise.

I really prefer being myself, she thought, *I don't really want to be anything else.*

The Miss Strega Owl stared at her with her big round eyes. Her head swivelled.

Jessica thought SCARY.

She thought of scary things, like ghosts in sheets making freaky hollers, or grizzly bears with large hairy claws, or sharks with double rows of sharp pointy teeth and whacking great tails.

To her surprise, Miss Strega suddenly hooted. Her feathery shoulders shook with laughter. Felicity stuffed a paw in her mouth and seemed to be choking. Berkeley was chirruping and hiccupping at the same time.

"Why are you all laughing?" protested Jessica. Then she caught the reflection of a strange creature in the window. It had the head of a ghost, a grizzly bear's fat tummy and a shark's tail.

She turned a little red. "This isn't a mistake. I'm just practising."

She concentrated hard. *Think scary*, she scolded herself. *Be serious.*

But she got it wrong again! Now she was another ridiculous monster with the big hammer nose of a shark, an empty ghostly middle and two huge paws with furry ankles where her own stripy socks should have been.

"Perhaps you can't do scary?" Miss Strega suggested.

Jessica's eyes narrowed. "Of course I can do scary."

"Perhaps you don't trust me to keep my Witch Switch Promise?"

Jessica bit her lip. "Of course I trust you."

She tried hard to think of something that would really scare Miss Strega.

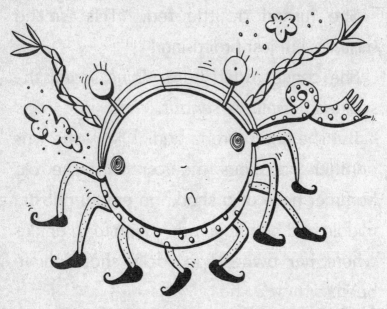

Jessica's eyes flashed and popped out on stalks. Steam poured out of her ears. She blew two long curling plumes of smoke through her nostrils. Her cheeks blazed. Her blood boiled. She swelled up to double her size. She sprouted one, two, three, four, five, six, seven, eight long, skinny, hairy legs. She skittered along the counter and glared at the owl with big, bulging eyes.

Miss Strega opened her mouth to yell the loudest yell ever heard.

Jessica crossed all her skinny legs and toes.

Please, please, Miss Strega, she was thinking, *keep your promise.*

"By the creaking neck bones of the snowy goose," she exclaimed, "that was scary! I do hate spiders, especially room-sized ones like that."

And there she was, sitting on her high stool, completely restored to Miss Strega shape. She patted her bun, rubbed her long chin, tapped the side of her nose  and smiled at Jessica over her half-moon glasses.

"Yes, everything seems to be back in working order. I'm one hundred per cent me. And you seem to be one hundred per cent you."

"Thank you for not letting me get stuck. I would absolutely *hate* to be a spider."

"It was very brave of you to do a spider Switch – you know how much I hate them - so thank you for trusting *me* to keep the Witch Switch Promise."

"You can trust me too – but can we just be ourselves now?"

"Absolutely, my little sugar plum. No more Witch Switches unless absolutely necessary."

Felicity gave a very loud relieved yawn and climbed on to the Spell Books for a nap. Berkeley flew back into Jessica's pocket and settled herself comfortably into the pocket fluff.

"There's just one thing, Miss Strega," said Jessica, chewing the end of her plait. "If you are clever enough to de-Switch and not be stuck as an owl, why have you left your great-aunt Delenda to be rained on for all this time?"

Miss Strega stroked her long chin. "My great-aunt who? All I can say, Jessica, is that if I did have a great-aunt Delenda who was silly enough to be caught out by her witch-in-training, then she would deserve to be left out in the cold."

Jessica turned a little red.

"But," added Miss Strega, "only Ordinary People expect trainees to get everything right first time round. Witches-in-training get second chances."

She nodded towards the trapdoor.

"Fancy a bit of a spin?" she asked.

"You bet," said Jessica.

They flew up on to the roof and hovered over the High Street. Below them, hundreds of Ordinary People were bustling in and out of the shops, queuing for buses, pushing babies in buggies, crashing about on skateboards. The bright neon lights of the shops winked and blinked.

Miss Strega looked down at her own little shop tucked in between the toy shop and the estate agent's.

"I'd better recast that spell on my shop, Jess, before we go any further," she said. "We don't want any more hugger-mugger with those Ordinary People."

She drew out her wand, sprinkled a handful of moondust down her chimneypot and began to chant.

"Shrink into the shadows.
Go back In Between.
By witches' eyes only
Are you to be seen."

Then Miss Strega stretched out her hand and took Jessica's. "Moonrays and marrowbones, all this Switching and Spelling has been exhausting. I think we both deserve a Moon-Vault."

And off they soared together, up and over the moon.

"Wey-hey!" they roared as they tumbled down the far side and Zoomed off for supper on the Milky Way.